MIRACLES
and
MAGIC

Pamela J. Olynek

BALBOA.
PRESS

A DIVISION OF HAY HOUSE

Balboa Press books may be ordered through booksellers or by contacting:

Balboa Press
A Division of Hay House
1663 Liberty Drive
Bloomington, IN 47403
www.balboapress.com
1 (877) 407-4847

Because of the dynamic nature of the Internet, any web addresses or
links contained in this book may have changed since publication and
may no longer be valid. The views expressed in this work are solely those
of the author and do not necessarily reflect the views of the publisher,
and the publisher hereby disclaims any responsibility for them.

The author of this book does not dispense medical advice or prescribe the use
of any technique as a form of treatment for physical, emotional, or medical
problems without the advice of a physician, either directly or indirectly. The
intent of the author is only to offer information of a general nature to help
you in your quest for emotional and spiritual well-being. In the event you use
any of the information in this book for yourself, which is your constitutional
right, the author and the publisher assume no responsibility for your actions.

Any people depicted in stock imagery provided by Thinkstock are models,
and such images are being used for illustrative purposes only.
Certain stock imagery © Thinkstock.

Print information available on the last page.

ISBN: 978-1-5043-3605-5 (sc)
ISBN: 978-1-5043-3606-2 (e)

Balboa Press rev. date: 8/10/2015

DEDICATION

TO LILLIAN

CONTENTS

BELIEVE

Long ago I started to write, as a child really, in the 1800's. I would get up in the night and put coal on the fire. I wore those fingerless gloves and boots while I wrote. The house was cold and damp. I lived in England.

I could hear mice down below in the kitchen, scurrying about looking for food. I had gotten used to them now. It was particularly cold tonight. I wrapped a scarf about my neck. I lived alone. My husband had died the year before of an illness. I was only 20, young still. I already knew I'd never marry again. So young to be widowed, though I was not the only one. A plaque had gone through, claiming many lives. I was selling a few children's books to provide for my basic necessities. My best time to write was in the night before the noise and clatter of the street at morning light. I was used to being up in the stillness and quiet of the night while everyone else slept. I rather liked hearing the beat of my own heart and the pen scratching the ink on the paper.

I was a somewhat tall lady and slender build. My long hair was braided and hung down my back. I sat at my desk and wrote.

I was walking along the forest path. All was quiet around me. I walked deeper and deeper into the forest. As I journeyed into the forest that night, my feet became tired and I laid down to rest. The morning light awoke me. The moss felt cool yet soft beneath me. I could hear the softest of voices around me. I lay still and listened."I wonder who she is.""What is she doing here?""She sure is big!""What a noisy sleeper she is!"

I realized then that I was the subject of this conversation. I decided to speak up. In my quietest of voices, I whispered, "Hello. I thank you for allowing me to sleep in your forest. I was so tired you see and needed to lay down. I hope I didn't interfere too much."I then waited and listened. You see I'd realized it was the fairies of the forest that I'd heard talking. I did not want to frighten them.

"All right then." I heard a scruff deep male voice this time. Must be a spokesman of sorts, I thought."I'd sure like to meet all of you." I whispered in response. There was much whispering amongst themselves. I waited and listened. My heart pounding with hope and excitement. For years now I had been reading about the fairy kingdom that resided out in nature. I had always felt drawn to them. I felt almost a kinship. This was the first time though that I had actually been amongst them! I awaited their response."Lillian has agreed to be seen by you. She's our brave one. A little like your Emma I daresay."I was taken aback. How did they know about Emma, my granddaughter? Lillian was so excited to meet a 'human being.' She'd always been so curious about them. Now here was her chance. I sat up now, choosing the traditional cross-legged Indian style. I waited expectantly."I'm over here," I heard the tiniest of voices.

I looked around me. Where was 'here?'"At the base of the tree, directly in front of you.""Oh my gosh!" I squealed. My hand immediately covered my mouth. I couldn't help myself. Those words just came flying out. There she was, the sweetest of creatures. Her tiny wings were aflutter. She wore the cutest lavender colored outfit. Her wings were the same shape and color as the two butterflies that were on the tree beside her. The wings were white with grey tips. There were four black dots placed symmetrically near the top of the wings. Lillian's hair was a shade of red that reminded me of my daughter's hair. It hung long beyond her shoulders. Her green eyes were large and twinkled with excitement. She had the cutest little nose and a broad smile. She had such sharp delicate facial features. She was so small yet so perfect, I thought.

Lillian fluttered about at the base of the tree, looking up into the face of this woman. She was nervous and excited. 'What now,' she thought. 'What's next.'"I've always wanted to meet a fairy. I'm so very grateful for this opportunity," I said aloud. "I'm so happy to finally meet you. Thank-you Lillian."She flew closer and higher until she was directly opposite my eye level."If you follow me, I'll show you something," she whispered to me and off she went through the trees. She raced ahead of me. I was surprised at how much distance she had already put between us. She would turn her head back over her shoulder occasionally to be certain I was still following her. Deeper and deeper into the forest we went. ' I hope I'll be able to find my way out,' I thought. Soon we came to a small clearing. I stopped and starred. Before me were what seemed like hundreds of fairies, big ones, little ones, baby ones, girl ones, boy ones. Ones that had the littlest of outfits with leaf shoes on their feet. Others had bare feet and leaf clothes and flowers in their hair. Looking and watching closer, it became apparent there were distinguishing groups of fairies, each with their own particular characteristics."What are they doing?" I asked Lillian."They are preparing for a very special ceremony," she answered. "We gather together every spring equinox. You have been blessed to come at this special time. You'll be able to witness it."I continued to watch as the many fairies busied themselves. Their little wings carried them from one place to the next. They appeared to be building something. Some kind of alter was what it seemed. They worked together in harmony like they instinctively knew what their specific task was. It was wonderful to watch. I stood in awe and wonder.

It was one thing to meet Lillian today and now here I was amidst more fairies than I could possibly count.

'What an amazing day this turned out to be,' I thought. The energy in this clearing was incredible! I could 'feel' it in the air. It was so strong. I started to feel 'strange' as I call it. Other times in my life I had felt this way. I recalled the time when I arrived on Vancouver Island and was about to take classes to get my Masters in Reiki. My mind began to wander back in time over the years that had brought me to now this time and this place. So much growth had taken place. So much wisdom had been gathered. So many blessings had been received. As I watched the fairies busily preparing for this special event, another part of me was transporting over time and space. It's like the strength of the energy in the meadow was causing this shift. Soon I was back at my desk in the cold damp house writing. My fingers gripping the pen were enclosed in the fingerless gloves in an attempt to keep them warm. Whenever I wrote though, I became so absorbed into my story that I no longer felt the cold. Whish! Whish! I could feel the flutter of the air movement from the fairy wings of Lillian as she went whisking past my face. She was so beautiful with her delicate features, her green eyes, her smile. I was back in the meadow. Lillian took off into the midst of the activity. "Stay right there," she yelled back over her shoulder. I took a seat on the mossy forest floor. I began to see just what they were building. It was a shrine after all. They were just finishing the alter part where gifts could be brought and laid at the base of the shrine. The entire thing was quite big actually, when you put it in perspective of their size. It was starting to become dusk. They'd have to stop soon. They quickened their pace. Obviously then their intention was to be done before dusk over took the sky completely. Lillian soon returned.

"It's time to go". It was starting to get dark now. I looked towards the trees. I could still see the outline of the forest path.

This was a good thing as I didn't have a flashlight. Up I got and once again Lillian led the way. Soon enough we were back where we started. "How is everything coming along?" the same husky voice asked. This was the one who had introduced me to Lillian many hours ago now. Lillian and he conversed a bit. I couldn't make out what they were saying. "Can I come back tomorrow?" I heard myself ask. "Can I attend the ceremony, the celebration for which they built the alter and shrine? I won't interfere. I won't bring anyone else with me. Nor will I tell anyone. It would sure mean a lot to me to witness this special event. I'd be very honored."They spoke amongst themselves again. They flew closer and fluttered up to my eye level."I can hear you wondering what my name is. It's Charles. I am the leader and organizer of this area of the forest. I keep an eye of sorts on the goings on in this part of the forest. We can see the aura of energy that surrounds you. It show us much more about you than any words you speak. We can see that you are indeed an honest soul and that we can trust you not to give away our secrets. It's not that we don't like humans. We do. They fascinate us just as much as we must fascinate you. However, we've observed their lack of respect for their earth, for their natural surroundings. We've come to know that we cannot trust them."

"Meet us here just before dusk tomorrow evening. The ceremony will start shortly after. Bring a candle or light of sorts for after dark just in case you lose sight of us." With that said, Lillian and Charles flew off. I turned and followed the path that led out of the forest. My heart and mind were racing, ' I don't know how much sleep I'll be able to get tonight,' I thought. That was amazing! Thank you God! Thank you so very much for that experience. I started to cry. Tears of joy and humility and gratitude flowed. I also felt this huge sense of relief.

'They are real!' I always knew in my heart they were – the fairy kingdoms. The big feeling of relief was because now I knew for sure. I had been given this incredible experience of validation. I felt honored and blessed. The next day couldn't come quick enough. Then once it did, I found myself eagerly watching the clock pass the needed hours away. This time I packed a light snack and brought a flashlight and sweater. As dusk drew, I headed back to the forest. Before long, I could hear Lillian's laughter and greeting.

"Hello my curious one. Did you get any sleep at all? "Not too much," I admitted. As dusk fell, all the meadow was lite up by fireflies dancing in the air providing 'candle light. 'I could hear the owls in the trees 'hooting' with excitement. All the animals of the forest were gathering around. What an amazing sight! Birds of all sizes and colors filled the branches of the trees. Sitting on the forest floor, were the rabbits and squirrels and chipmunks and even the little mice. It was like a silent truce had been called between natural predators for all sat and gathered together. There was this incredible energy of Peace and Love. This same energy surrounded me. It was so strong. I was reminded of those rare occurrences in my personal life when I'd been blessed to experience such energy as this.

The creatures of the forest continued to gather. Bambi's as I call the baby deer, were amongst them. Being spring some of the young ones had been born. Other females were big with babies soon to arrive. Even crickets gathered and began singing their songs of praise. Butterflies flittered about and colourful moths. A few wolves and a fox or two watched from a distance through the trees. It looked as though the fairies were getting prepared to make a fire. They must have worked many hours to have gathered all the sticks and small pieces of wood that were now in the sunken center of this rock.

Its position caused the setting sun to shine on it in such a way as to gather enough heat to start a flame. This flame grew bigger and bigger. The animals gathered around this huge rock. As the fairies did the same, I felt a 'Spirit Energy' envelope me! It reminded me of a time years prior when I felt the most amazing sensation of Love Energy wrapping around me.' I really have had the most incredible Spirit experiences,' I thought. I had been sitting back on the grass by the edge of the trees. This way I was able to take in the whole scene: the animals as they had been gathering, the fairies as they had been busily preparing for this spring equinox ceremony and the fireflies as they fluttered about like dancing candle lights.

Now however, it was darker and the flame on the huge rock was growing larger and brighter, casting shadows. I decided to move in closer. I had no idea where Lillian was. As I moved, I prayed I wouldn't startle any of the fairies. I so wanted to witness this celebration of theirs. The fairies came together and formed a circle around the huge rock. Their wings fluttered to keep them off the ground. They began to sing.

"Dear God above in Heaven so High. Please join us now in Prayer and Light."The fireflies continued to dance about at the edge of the forest, creating a circle of light behind us. All of a sudden there was this 'silence' among everyone as if something great and majestic was about to happen. The 'silence' held great respect. All the fairies began speaking aloud in unison."We are gathered here this night to pay homage and respect to our meadow and to our world. We have much to be grateful for. Let us pray.""Dear God Above please hear our prayers this night and all nights. Please know that our tiny hearts are filled with awe and gratitude at Your Amazing Universe. We love You so and feel very blessed by You. We truly do live in an 'Enchanted Forest.' Thank you for the animals and birds and butterflies and all the other living things surrounding us.

We understand that each have a part in making our forest as wondrous as it is. We ask for Your Blessing upon us on this special night of the Spring Equinox. We pray for this coming summer to be filled with much joy and beauty. The flowers are beginning to bloom and the new leaves are filling the branches of the trees. May we continue to hear and follow Your Guidance each and every day. May we continue to live in peace and harmony with each other and with Your Universe. We pray this in Your Name Father. Amen."Their little voices sounded so magical and powerful as they recited the prayer. I sat and reflected on what I had just witnessed. It seemed strange to hear 'fairies' pray. 'But why shouldn't they?' I heard my Inner Voice reply. 'For like humans they too are creations of God. And they too are aware of this. Dark was fuller upon us now. The fire roared as bright colorful flames danced and rose up above the rock. 'What was next,' I wondered. The evening was pleasantly warm. The sky was filled with stars. Suddenly Angels of Light appeared. Big beautiful angels, all aglow, hovered above the fire. Once again I could feel the energy change in the air all around me. Even the hairs on my arms stood up! Next I sensed hands on my shoulders. I heard a whisper in my ear. "Welcome, Pamela! We are pleased that you are here!"I turned and looked behind me. No one was there. I resumed to view, what I was now calling, 'My Night with the Fairies. 'I felt so honored to be allowed to be here. I knew in my heart this was only granted on special occasions to a select few. I had always believed in the 'Magical Kingdom of Fairies.' I'd always prayed for a time when I could see one. Now here I was amidst so many fairies and now angels too! It was beyond words, the emotions I felt. I was embraced in love by the Angels. I, in turn, felt love for each and every one of the fairies.

I knew they were 'good. ' I saw that they lived in harmony and peace with each other and with the nature that surrounded them. An Angel spoke," I am Celeste. I have come here tonight to thank each of you for being true to your heart, for it is in living from the heart that creates places such as these." The second Angel spoke. "I am Larrisa. I thank you for your prayers of love and gratitude. It is in living with gratitude that maintains a continued flow of prosperity and well being to your villages." Then the third Angel spoke. "My name is Mayfair. We are very happy to come here tonight as you join in groups to celebrate." She raised her hand and upon opening it sprinkled 'Fairy Dust' over their villages. The magical twinkling sparkles shimmered in the moonlight as they fell to the ground and onto the fairies themselves. Some fell on me as well. It was like receiving an Energy Session in one touch. Immediately, I felt my vibrational field elevated and as I looked around me all the colors now seemed brighter and more vivid. I saw colors I'd never seen before. Like the one I was looking at now a shade somewhere between blue and orange. The fairies were all chatting about now. I listened yet could not understand them. They spoke so softly and quickly. I felt myself rising from where I'd been sitting. Everyone was moving about now. I looked at the sky. Dawn would be soon. 'How had so much time passed?' I wondered. 'Had I fallen asleep?' My body did feel a bit stiff and definitely in need of a stretch. "Come over here," I heard Lillian say. I followed along the path. Her tiny wings led the way shimmering and sparkling as they fluttered ahead of me. I could hear the waterfall before I saw it. "Wow! This is incredible," I exclaimed. "I never knew this was here." Lilian had led me to an opening at the edge of the forest that now revealed a large cascading waterfall.

I continued to follow her. She was leading me up to the fall itself. Next she led me around behind it. "Be careful, the rocks are slippery," she yelled back at me. How thoughtful of her to warn me so I was safe. 'Where is she taking me now,' I wondered. We stopped for a bit. As I stood there and looked out through the back of the waterfall, the mist shimmered through the now morning sunlight. This created a wonderful rainbow in front of us. 'So beautiful,' I thought to myself. 'So very, very beautiful.' The mist felt cool and refreshing. I followed the line of the rainbow with my eyes. Where it ended against the rock was a cave entrance. "Lillian, are we headed over to that cave?" I asked her. "Yes," she responded back. "There's someone there who wants to meet you." 'Who could that be,' I wondered. I was excited and curious and not the least bit afraid. I knew in my heart that in the fairies world I would always be safe and that only good would occur. We made our way towards the cave entrance. It was further than it looked and took us several minutes. I asked Lillian. "Who are we meeting in the cave?" "Our Fairy God-Mother," she answered. We were now at the cave's entrance. "I will wait for you here," Lillian said. The path inside led downwards on a slope. The walls were made of crystal. The sun shone on them lighting my way. Soon I stood at an opening to a large room also made of crystal. Sparkling light from the crystalline surface filled the room. I stood at the entrance in awe and wonder at this incredible sight. 'Pure Magic,' I thought. 'That's what lives here-Pure Magic!'

I then realized that across from me was another opening.
Now moving from that opening into the cave was the most
beautiful queen like fairy I could ever imagine. Such grace
and loving energy emanated from her. I use the word 'fairy'
yet she was adult human size. Her eyes, as she looked across
to me, were the deepest and richest color of blue. Her hair
was long and blond and flowing down her back. A crown,
adorned with crystals, sat atop her head. Her large wings
reminded me of peacock feathers. They had the same design
of oval shaped patterns on the wings' tips. Her embroidered
gown appeared to be made of silk and flowed to the floor.
She held in her hand a wand of sorts with a star shape at
the end. It looked to be made of crystal also. She continued
to move into the center of the cave. "Welcome," she spoke in
the clearest of voices. "Come into the cave more. I want to see
you." I moved towards this image of beauty before me. I felt
all tingly from being amongst this intense crystal energy. I
felt light headed and as if my feet weren't even touching the
ground. It reminded me of when I go to my favorite book store
in the city that has huge crystals amidst the room. "I am the
Fairy God-Mother. I am so pleased to meet with you. Come. We
can sit over here." I looked to where she pointed and realized
there were two seats formed right into the crystal. We sat down
simultaneously. She reached out and took both my hands into
hers. She looked into my eyes and spoke. "We, the fairies and
I, are so glad to have you with us. We realize it all must seem
rather overwhelming for you. We have felt your passion and
love for our world. We can see in your heart that you mean us
no harm. There is an opportunity available here and now for
you to consider. You see, my dear Pamela, if you choose it, I can
use my magic powers to change your physical form into that
of a fairy!" 'What did she just say? Did I hear her correctly?
Of all the things I thought might be spoken here today

that never occurred to me.' "Become a fairy myself?" I exclaimed aloud in my bewilderment. "Yes," she answered. "It would only be for a short while – not permanent. The fairies have let me know of their willingness to allow you this experience. This is indeed a great honor and should be looked at in this manner. Only a very few humans over the ages, have been invited to actually enter fully into the fairy world by becoming similar in appearance and size themselves. On this day, this honor and privilege is being offered to you." I started to sweat. My palms were moist. My heart was beating fast with anticipation. "Yes!" I cried out. "Yes please. I do accept, with so much gratitude, this truly amazing opportunity." "Let us bow our heads in prayer, my child," she said. Simultaneously, she placed the tip of her wand ever so gently on my crown chakra at the top of my head. "Dear God above," she began. "Please hear our prayer. We ask for You to bless this day what is about to transpire here. We ask that you would lay Your hand upon Pamela's body and transform it with Your Grace into the fairy form. May she in Spirit remain true to herself within this new shape. May she continue to feel Your Love so strong in her soon to be tiny heart. May her new wings carry her safely into the world of the fairies. Our intention is for her to see the beauty and joy that exists there. May she continue to trust You explicitly with her faith of a child. Amen." In the length of time it took for her to speak aloud that prayer, my body indeed had been transformed. I felt the same. I felt like my 'Self.' Yet when I looked down at my feet, I saw tiny ones. When I looked across at the woman who had been holding my hands, I realized I was now 'fluttering' in mid air before her!! 'This is weird!' I thought to myself. I could feel the oddest of sensations on my back. It was my 'wings ' fluttering back and forth. All of a sudden, I felt absolutely EXHILARATED!!

"I can fly! I can fly!" I exclaimed. "Lillian. Lillian. Come and see," I cried out. I moved about the cave in darting gestures. I headed towards the entrance to the cave to find Lillian. "Have fun," I heard the Magical Lady behind me cry aloud. "I will meet you back here when the time is right. You'll know when that is." I fluttered my wings back up the slope to the entrance. 'This is too cool,' I thought to myself. 'Oh my Oh my I can hardly believe this is really happening.' I felt EXHILARATED that is the word that best describes it. I felt excited and amazed and in a state of awe and wonder all at the same time. "There you are," Lillian was in front of me now. I stopped and stood on the rock before the wall of mist from the waterfall. I needed to catch my breath for a minute. "You look amazing!" Lillian exclaimed. "I'm so glad you said yes. I have so much I want to show you." I followed Lillian back the way we had come behind the waterfall and over the wet slippery rocks only this time I was above them flying! "This is amazing!" I shouted aloud, wanting her to hear me above the sound of the waterfall. Everything had a different 'feel' to it somehow. Of course, in 'view' all was different but there was something else as well. I couldn't quite put my finger on it. "Look here," Lillian said. We had stopped by a calm pool of water a distance from the waterfall. I looked down at my reflection in the water. I was speechless. "See how beautiful and natural looking a fairy you've become," Lillian exclaimed. Before me, in the glass like mirror image this is what I saw. On the top of my head was a headband made of Lily of the Valley's bell shaped flowers. My hair, now long and golden in color, flowed down my back. I had bare feet. My outfit was the color of the sun, a little sleeveless top and matching long skirt. The material was soft against my skin. I turned my neck as far as possible to catch a glimpse of my new 'wings.' They stretched out behind me, the colors shimmering in their reflection in the water. Their shape reminded me of dragon fly's wings. I could barely feel them. It was like asking someone if they felt their skin. As I gazed down at my image in the pond, I began to flutter my wings. Soon I was airborne. It all happened so effortlessly. I didn't have to consciously think about it. It would be like me picking up a pen and starting to write. I just 'did' it. Well, in the same way, my wings fluttered back and forth whenever I wanted. "This is a lot for you to take in all at once," Lillian said as I continued to stare at my reflection in the water. "Let's sit on this rock over here for a bit and take a short break." I followed her to a smooth rock she'd noticed by the water's edge. We both settled down upon it. Sitting now side by side each of equal size, we looked back at the distant waterfall. After some time had passed, Lillian turned to me and spoke, "I think I'm going to call you Jester." "Jester?" I asked. "Why?" "It's time for you to have some fun and magic in your life. The name Jester has that vibration." Lillian answered back. "Come on. It's time to go," she added as she stood up on the rock. "Follow me." Off she went. "Wait up," I called after her. She led me back towards the forest, and away from the waterfall and the crystal cave. 'Jester, what an odd name,' I thought as I followed behind her. I felt excited and yet nervous at the same time. Where was she taking me now, I wondered. All of a sudden, I could smell the most beautiful flowers. It was like roses and lilies and lavender all mixed together. Lillian had led me into an amazing garden. I noticed other fairies here too.

There was such a variety of them, each different and unique yet similar, like people. "I want to rest here for a while Lillian. I want to stop and be amongst the flowers and the other fairies." Lillian came to rest by the edge of a fish pond. "It's so beautiful here," I said as I settled down beside her. "Tell me about yourself Lillian. Tell me about the fairy kingdom." I eagerly awaited her response. "Well, the first thing you should know is that the fairies have been here on Planet Earth as long as the humans have been. It's just that the majority of people walk right by and don't even notice we're here. They are too absorbed in their own thoughts and their own lives. Also, most humans have a much lower vibration so they wouldn't be able to see us anyways. They eat too much processed food and watch too much violence on their television sets. All these things lower ones' vibration. As a result, a lot of people miss out on the miracles and magic of everyday life. We are not a lot different than you, Jester. It's just that we understand the Laws of this Universe and we live by them. We understand there is a God and that Love is a powerful Energy Force, not just a word. The Fairy Kingdom is a peacefull and joyful one. We love life and are grateful for all its beauty. We see beauty in each other as well. We are tolerant of our differences. We recognize and acknowledge one another's strengths. We use positive language when we speak, for we understand the power of our words. We also understand that our thoughts are energy, so we've learned to monitor them and keep them positive and loving. We sat side by side in silence for a bit reflecting on what had been said. "Wow look at that huge butterfly!" I exclaimed. The largest butterfly I had ever seen just landed on a nearby flower. "It's a Monarch," I shouted aloud. "Just like my tattoo!" I looked down at my arm then, remembering that I was no longer of "human" form. Did my tattoo remain with me during my transformation? I looked at my, now tiny arm and yes, sure enough, there was my tattoo of a monarch butterfly,

I turned to look at the real live Monarch now sipping the flower's nectar. What a different perspective things were now that I was fairy size. The Monarch was as big as I, or vice versa, depending on how one looked at it. I could actually see the creature to whom those beautiful orange and black wings belonged. I turned away from that sight and glanced over the garden as a whole. Flowers and fairies were everywhere. There were flowers of every color and shape and size. As I looked closer, I soon realized that there was a connection between each fairy and each flower. Just as the flowers in the garden were diverse with so many varieties, so too the fairies were many and varied in their statue and dress. Closer inspection soon revealed that each flower had one or more corresponding fairy flying around it. These flower fairies were outfitted in clothing that precisely matched the flower's colors and design. It was all so Divinely orchestrated, so Perfect, so Magnificent!! I continued to stare at this incredible sight. Another thing I noticed, was the youthful looks of the fairies and their childlike manner. "It's true then," I said aloud. "Another author's drawings of flower fairies is accurate. It's all true! I always thought they were so beautiful and so incredible. Yet here it is. Right here in front of me!" I could hardly believe it. It was like a dream, like a 'fairy' tale. Hmm. Interesting choice of words that expression. I'd have to ponder that more later. Right now I jumped to my tiny feet and fluttered my delicate beautiful wings. I started to go from flower to flower introducing myself to the other fairies. "Hello. I'm Jester. I'm so happy to meet you. You are so beautiful!" "Hey! Flower Fairies! Lillian shouted. "Let's play a game of Hide and Seek with Jester." Soon all the fairies were gathered around Lillian and I. Excitement filled the air. "Yes! Yes! Let's play," they replied. They began to divide themselves into teams. Lillian explained the game to me. Her and I joined one of the teams. Pretty soon we were all flying about laughing and squealing with delight. Each group looked for a good hiding spot in the garden. Once everyone was settled in and quiet, Lillian, through her intention and her thoughts, invited in Charles to join them in this game.(Charles, if you remember, was the male fairy who was with Lillian when they found me in the forest.) From where Lillian and I were hiding, I could soon see Charles arrive. "Look out! Look out! Wherever you are. I'll soon be finding you. Beware! Beware! He shouted out playfully for all to hear. Little snickers could be heard here and there around the garden. Oh what fun we had all that afternoon! "It's time for us to go now," Lillian said. I stood and spoke aloud to the group. "I had so much fun. Thank you for playing with me. I'll never forget our time together. Bye! Bye!" I waved as I hurried to catch up to Lillian. Lillian came to rest on a rock by a little creek. Flowers grew by the water's edge. "Let's rest a bit," Lillian said. I felt such immense joy and gratitude at this magical opportunity I'd been given. I flew from flower to flower embraced in each moment's gift of wonder. The scents of the flowers enveloped me as I entered their space. What an incredible experience to be able to fly right into the center of a rose and then a lily. I landed my little feet on the flower's petal. I put out my now tiny hand and stroked its velvety surface. I sat down on one. Lillian soon joined me. "Why me? Why am I being given this wondrous experience?" I asked aloud. "You have been awarded this time with us spontaneously. For as you happened to come across our path on your walk, we could sense your gentleness of spirit. We knew in our hearts that you would never hurt us nor betray us. We knew you would always honor our privacy and not disclose our Kingdom location."

"It's okay to write about my experience here though isn't it?" I asked. "Absolutely!" Lillian exclaimed. "We want people, especially the children, to know about us. Our wish would be that as they grow into adults, they would continue to believe. It saddens our hearts when we watch so many walk right by us, unable to see us because they no longer believe. Perhaps, if they did believe they'd stop dropping their garbage along the pathways" We sat in silence for a bit. "What do you eat in the Fairy Kingdom? I'm getting hungry even though I am so tiny now," I exclaimed. "Follow me," Lillian answered and off she went. Within a few minutes we were back at her village. She stopped in front of one of the wee houses. "Come on in." As I followed her in, I thought 'Wow, this is cool. I can fit inside these now.' I had two decorative 'fairy ' houses on a tabletop at home. Inside this one was the tiniest table and chair set I could possibly ever imagine. All of it was made from pieces of wood. They were held together by a sticky sap they'd gathered in the fall, Lillian explained. In one corner, on another table, was what appeared to be a bowl holding pieces of fruit. Lillian brought it over to the table as she sat down beside me. "Let us pray." Lillian bowed her head and continued. "Dear God, thank you for this food and thank you for my new friend and this amazing day we are sharing together. Amen." "Amen," I echoed. "Other members of the village prepared this feast of fruit for us. Help yourself," said Lillian. "Thank you," I replied. My mind attempted to grasp all the steps that must have transpired to have before me now this delicious and nutritious meal of fruit. I was about to ask Lillian about what those steps might be, when I heard "Let's just enjoy it." from Lillian. She seemed to know what I was about to ask.

I could hear music in the background. We left the little house and flew up an incline. At the top, I saw a gathering of fairies in the meadow below. "That's where the music is coming from," I exclaimed. "It's sing song time in the meadow." Lillian said. "Do you know how long I'll be here, in your Fairy Kingdom? Do you know exactly why I'm here? Lillian, is there special purpose for all this happening to me?" I asked, wanting to continue our earlier conversation. "Let's sit down over here and talk about this further," Lillian said as she showed me the way to a small group of trees. Well, to us they looked like trees. I guess in human form, they'd be more like a few sparse looking shrubs or clumps of grass really. We sat down there, away from the others. "We want you to write a book about us," Lillian began. "We want you to remind people of the beauty and magical wonder of the Fairy Kingdom. We want people to believe in us again. We know they are ready now to truly hear about the miracles and wonders of nature and life. People are opening their hearts and minds and looking at things outside the 'normal' way that they had been taught. We have received clear signs that now is the time for us to make ourselves known again. We spent a lot of time and thought and prayer on this. Then, so perfectly you appeared, like a sign. Will you write about us?" Lillian looked at me expectantly. "Of course I will." I answered. "I'd be honored to." "Great. I knew you'd say yes." She replied. "Come on. There's something I want to show you." Off she went ahead of me. "Wait up," I yelled after her. 'Here we go again,' I thought to myself. I was so happy and excited by what she has just said. Also, I was eager to see what else she wanted to show me.

I saw the castle before the rainbow. Yet even before those, I 'felt' the energy field around me change drastically and abruptly. It was like what I would have imagined to feel like if one suddenly entered a portal into a different time zone. Initially, I felt the sensation of walking through a doorway made of a jelly like substance. I had to push myself through with more added effort than usual. The colors were amazing! Whether it be the green of the meadow surrounding the castle or the purple of the flowers or the blue of the sky, all the colors were more vibrant and aglow. Lillian flew in front of me. I followed as I looked around trying to take it all in. "Stupendous!" That's the word that came to my mind. "Absolutely stupendous!" I declared aloud. A rainbow displaying all the wondrous colours arched over the castle. Lillian kept leading us closer and closer. Then when we were about thirty feet away, she stopped and motioned for me to do the same. "Grandmother Fairy lives here," she explained. "You have been invited to visit with her. She is very beautiful and filled with such Grace!" I listened intently as she spoke. I didn't want to miss a word. "It is indeed a great honor for you to be invited to her castle. Usually when Grandmother Fairy meets with us, she comes to our villages and visits with us there. Let's carry on now. I am very excited for you." Once again Lillian flew off ahead with I close behind her. Within minutes, we were at the castle door. The castle itself was a creamy white color with blotches of grey. It was very old. In fact, I'm sure it had been there for centuries and more. I could not make out the exact material that made up its great walls. I only knew instinctively that the materials were from Mother Nature herself. It looked just like the castles you see in books, tall and majestic and turrets at the top. There was no moat or draw bridge in front though, just the colorful meadow that led right up to the door. No flag symbol hung to represent the owner either. Rather the castle was within the arch of the most brilliant rainbow I'd ever seen. Lillian tapped ever so gently on the large castle door. Within seconds, the door was opened by the most beautiful blue winged fairy. Tall and so serene looking, she held open the door wide for us to enter. "Hello. My name is Stephena. Grandmother Fairy has been expecting both of you." Now when one looked at the outside walls of the castle, one would automatically think that the inside would also look ancient in texture and appearance. This however was not the case. Inside was like walking into a beautiful magical garden. Birds sang their sweet songs. Colorful butterflies flew about the flower beds. Water made soothing sounds as it cascaded down a rocky slope. I looked up and could see the sky above us. I realized now, the walls only gave the illusion of an old fortress. "Wait here," said Stephana. She quickly returned. "Follow me." This time she rose up and flew. We followed in suit, our tiny wings fluttering away to keep up with her larger ones. She took us up to the top level of the castle wall. There appeared a loft shaped room. Stephena set herself down. Lillian and I did the same. There, sitting on a throne encompassed by flowers was Grandmother Fairy. She radiated Light in all directions. This beautiful Grandmother Fairy was almost iridescent. Remember earlier, I had said the flower fairies were so young and childlike. Well, in that same context then, Grandmother Fairy was a 'mature' fairy (like we would thing of a grown woman in human terms.) She was dressed in a flowing pink gown. She had golden hair that fell in waves all down her back. Her wings were the same color as her gown and the flowers that surrounded her throne. Her crown, that fit like a headband, was made from the flowers' golden stamens. I immediately felt enveloped in this incredible circle of peace and calm. I could not speak. I was still trying to comprehend all of it. She spoke first. "Come sit closer here by me on these stools. I understand you have come a very long way through time and space to visit us my dear Pamela. "It is a great honor and privilege to be here, I know," I said. "I am so very humbled and grateful for this opportunity. I am eager to learn about the fairy kingdom that I may one day write about it to share this amazing experience with others." "I can see in your heart that you mean us no harm,' she said." And that your intentions are pure. Lillian is the perfect guide for you. I know she will show you around well enough. Let's eat and replenish after your journey." Stephana soon appeared with leaf bowls filled with nuts and fruit. We ate and laughed as Grandmother Fairy shared some stories. The best story of all was when she explained how long ago she had lived in author Cecily Barker's flower garden. That to me was truly amazing! Now here I was visiting with the very same fairy a hundred years later. Surely then, the Fairy Kingdom operated under a totally different concept of time than us humans. How thrilled and excited I was to have her refer to the author that had the same passion for fairies as myself and whose works I was very familiar with. This connection, in itself, was magical. Needless to say, our evening visit passed all too quickly. The next morning, as we stood at the castle door saying our goodbyes, I looked across the meadow and saw a Unicorn!! "Oh, my God, a real live Unicorn!" I exclaimed. "Isn't she beautiful?" Grandmother Fairy responded. "She even allows me to ride on her on occasion." "I will never forget this visit," I told her. "Thank you for allowing me to come here." "May the rest of your time in Fairy Land be just as wonderful," she shouted after us as we flew away.

Upon returning to the village, I found myself beginning to wonder how much time I had left in this fairy body and in this Fairy Kingdom. I was starting to feel that it would soon be time to leave. I sat back and looked around me, at their village. I pondered the lives they led. I asked myself, 'What did I see? What did I notice? What did I feel? The energy of the village was light, happy, and joyful and there was a deep peace and strength. The fairies went about their day with the sound of laughter between them. They moved as one unit whenever there was a major task to accomplish. They spoke only positive, encouraging words. They played like children. What would it be like to be raised in such a place, I wondered. Lillian came and sat beside me. "You look deep in thought," she said. "I am beginning to sense that I'll be leaving soon," I responded. "So I was taking a moment to look over your village and the activity. "We have so much to tell you," Lillian said. "So much to teach and share so that you will come to understand the Fairy Kingdom. Most of all we want people to believe that there is so much beauty and magic and wonder and joy to be experienced every single day. It's always there, every day. One needs only to experience a change of perception first. To do that requires a healing of the heart, a healing from within." Lillian continued, "We are aware of the pressures and stresses of the modern technological world humans live in. It's time to step aside from that. It's time to play and laugh and heal and grow within. It's time to put one's spiritual journey to the forefront of one's goals and ambitions. It's time to also learn the art of manifestation and allowing. You are each the creator of your own experience. More and more of you are learning this now. This is very exciting for us to see. Like yourself, for example, each day you are witness to your own creation. It takes you by surprise still as you continue to learn the power of your own thoughts."

I sat engrossed in her words. Lillian continued. "You have truly uncovered the magic of daily living and are experiencing joy-filled days. We have enjoyed meeting with you and spending time with you. It will soon be time for you to return back to your human shape. Again we tell you, we give permission to share of your experience with us, though not yet our Kingdom location." "Come I'll show you the way back to the waterfall and Fairy God-Mother. She will change you back to your original form," Lillian concluded. I had listened to every word Lillian had spoken, engraving it in my mind to draw upon in detail later. Right now I 'fluttered' my wings and followed her through the forest. I could soon hear the waterfall in the distance. As we approached, I yelled aloud to Lillian, "Can we stop at the waterfall? I'd love to sit and enjoy this view before I go." "Of course," Lillian replied. As we settled on a rock, I took in my surroundings. I could feel the spray coming from the waterfall on my tiny arms and legs. I felt confused yet in awe at this entire experience. I felt like I'd been a fairy for many days. I had the strangest feeling that when I went back to my human life that I'd discover that only a few hours had passed. I looked over to Lillian. She was looking back at me. "I'll miss you," I spoke aloud. "I know," she replied. "And I you. This was a very unusual experience for me as well. I know you'll do right by us when it comes time for you to share of your adventure here. Who knows, perhaps you will be allowed to come and visit us again. Until then, we will remain joined in our hearts, for once there has been a connection there, it is never broken."

Just then a beautiful Monarch butterfly landed on the rock beside us. "She is telling us that it's time to go. She is also saying that henceforth, each time you see a Monarch Butterfly, it will be a reminder to you of the existence of the fairy realm and your time spent with us," Lillian explained. It seemed perfectly natural that she had communicated with the Monarch butterfly. We arose and fluttered our tiny wings. We travelled once again behind the waterfall. Soon we were at the entrance to the 'magical' cave. "I have to say good-bye to you here," Lillian spoke. As I looked into her tiny sweet face, I could feel tears filling my eyes. She placed her hand on my heart. "Remember, I'll always be right here," she said. Lillian then placed something in my hand. I looked down. My eyes sparkled with joy and surprise. In my hand, she had placed a perfect ornamental replica of herself! "Something for your desk at home," she said. "I carved it." I hugged her tiny frame with mine. "Thank you. Thank you so much. I'll treasure it always," I said. "Bye," she called out as she began to head back toward the front of the waterfall. "Bye Lillian," I yelled after her. "Bye." I turned to enter the cave. My heart was no longer sad. Instead, I felt joyful with gratitude. I fluttered my tiny wings and went further into the cave. Soon I came to the central larger area. I looked around and saw no one. I felt so small and tiny in my fairy form in this huge crystal cave. I saw the two seats molded into the crystal where Fairy God-Mother and I had sat before. I saw the opposite entrance to the cave from whence she had entered last time. I wondered when she would arrive. No sooner had I finished that thought, then I could feel her energy before I even saw her form.

I was already tingly and lightheaded from being amidst all the crystal. "How are you Pamela dear?" She spoke in the clearest of voices. "How was your time with Lillian?" She seemed to float into the cave. Her long blond hair flowed behind her. Her blue eyes sparkling as she looked at me. "Come over here, closer to me." She took a seat in one of the crystal chairs. I flew over and came to rest on the arm of the seat beside her. "Was your fairy adventure all you hoped it to be?" she asked. "Oh, yes!" I exclaimed. "It was wonderful, breathtaking and magical! Lillian was the perfect guide and a great friend. I think I'm still spellbound by this whole experience. I'll be processing all that's happened for days to come I'm sure." "Are you ready to change back now to your human shape and size?" the Fairy God-Mother asked. She seemed so giant like, talking to me, while I was still in this fairy form. Her energy was so loving and peaceful. Her voice was so soft and gentle. I felt safe. "I loved being in the fairy kingdom," I replied. "If I ever had to choose between the human world and the fairy's, I'd pick theirs. It was so peaceful and beautiful and harmonious. There was no displaced anger or jealousy or lying or other negative hurtful behaviour. Everyone worked together and yet acknowledged the individual connectedness to the whole. They worked and functioned as one unit and all benefited. It was wonderful to see and to witness." "Ah, it sounds like you allowed yourself to open your heart and truly feel what it is like to be a fairy," she responded. "It is because of this, that you will be able to write of your visit here. Your words will be felt as well as heard. Such words will open the doors of many human hearts. More will come to believe in the fairies. This will be a beneficial thing for all."

"Are you ready for me to change you back now Pamela?" she asked again. "Could I just do one more quick fly around?" I asked her, surprising myself. The question had just blurted out of me. "I so have enjoyed these wings," I continued. "Absolutely, please do," she replied. "I'll just do a quick look at the waterfall again," I answered. Off I went. My colorful wings carried me forward and through the entrance to the cave. Soon I felt the mist of the waterfall on my tiny face and arms. I flew behind the waterfall for a few minutes, taking in the beauty of it all. The way the spray of the water and the sunlight met, created a rainbow over the pond out front. 'Oh, how I love rainbows!,' I thought. How perfect that I got to see one here again. It would soon be time to go. I was now okay with that. I flew around to the front of the waterfall. I found a rock ledge along the side and decided to sit for a bit. I wanted to remember every detail of these surroundings. I was already looking forward to capturing it all on paper. I was so grateful and honored to receive permission to write about my adventures among the fairies. My prayer is that I do right by them. They said I could return. Perhaps I would show them what I've written before I send it off to be published. Wow! That's a great idea. With that thought in mind, I arose and fluttered my strong, reliable yet tiny wings. I headed back behind the waterfall towards the cave. Fairy God-Mother was still seated in the crystal chair. Her eyes were closed. She appeared to be deep in meditation. "I heard your thoughts," she said as she opened her eyes. "Yes that would be a perfect time to revisit, when your manuscript is done. We will go over it together. Then, I can be sure all is as it's meant to be. I'm sure it will be. That is why you have been chosen for this task. Come closer my dear. It's time." I flew closer and sat on the edge of her chair. I looked up into her beautiful blue eyes.

They shone so bright and so full of love. I felt embraced in their warmth. Once again, she placed the star shaped tip of her crystal wand on my crown chakra at the top of my head. She began, "By the Power invested in me, I do hereby return you, Pamela, back to your original human form. May all your fairy experiences be held forever in your heart." I felt a tingling sensation throughout my being. Then in the next second, I was sitting in my full human sized form in the crystal seat beside Fairy God-Mother. I just sat silent for a few moments. I was adjusting physically and emotionally to being back in my human sized body. The first thing I noticed and missed, were my wings. "I miss my wings," I spoke aloud. "I'm sure you do, my sweet child," she responded. She leaned over and took my hands in hers. Her touch felt so comforting and soothing. "I want you to remember something Pamela. I want you to remember that you have the truest wings of all. Those are the 'Wings of Spirit.' We must first open our hearts to life and to all of its magic and miracles and wonder. Then we must have faith and believe in things we cannot see. Then we are able to 'fly' to heights and have 'spirit' experiences beyond words. You, Pamela, have had such experiences. You have an open heart. You do believe in miracles and magic and the spirit realm. So Pamela, even though you may now not have your 'fairy' wings, your true 'Wings of Spirit' will always be with you." I listened intently. Fairy God-Mother was reminding me of my 'true wings.' 'Wings of the Heart' is what I liked to call it. I felt renewed strength and confidence as I listened to her words. Knowing who I was in my heart and having such strong conviction in my beliefs, I would indeed continue to 'fly' in many miraculous moments.

I rose from my seat. I knelt down before her. I looked up into her beautiful face and into those compassionate eyes. I felt a tear slide down my cheek. "Thank you. Thank you so very much for allowing me this magical experience. I will indeed treasure it in my heart always." "We will meet again Pamela, my dear. Until that time, may your angels and guides continue to watch over you, keeping you safe and guiding your Path." She bent forward and kissed my cheek. I closed my eyes. When I opened them again, she was gone. I arose and exited the cave. Back out into the sunshine, I made my way around the back of the waterfall. Then, I walked around the pond and back onto the forest path. I turned around for one last look. 'What!!' Behind me was only more forest and a path. Gone was the waterfall!! Gone was the sparkle of the crystal cave entrance. Gone was the pond and the waterfall mist and the rainbow. All of it vanished!! Now all I saw were trees and the forest path. I stood there for several minutes trying to comprehend what my eyes were 'not' seeing. The Fairy World was no longer visible to me. I took a few deep breaths and I turned and began to walk. This path would lead me out of the forest and home. The sun felt warm on my face. I could hear the birds in the trees. It was still a beautiful day and I was grateful for it. Suddenly, a Monarch butterfly darted in front of me, startling me. It continued to fly just ahead of me as I walked along. I remembered what Lillian had said about how the Monarch now would be of special significance, a reminder of our time together. I smiled at the magic and wonder of the butterfly's appearance at just this precise time! I then opened my hand and there, in my palm, was the gift Lillian had made for me. I started to laugh and cry at the same time. 'Yes indeed,' I thought. 'Fairies are definitely real!' I quickened my step on the path home. Ideas for this fairy story were already dancing about in my head.

ALWAYS WITH YOU

As I sat at my desk, pen in hand, I felt rather forlorn. Things were not moving as quickly as I'd hoped for my finished book on the fairies. Yes, I had returned that day, back in human form once again. I had eagerly arrived home, ideas and words already forming in my head. I was so excited to be able to write a story of my recent amazing experiences amongst the fairies. Now, a year later the book was completed. I'd done my own editing. I had no illustrator. So it seemed perfectly fitting to add in a few of another author's fairy drawings. I had received positive feedback from the few people I'd asked to read my story. They were delighted with it. I was encouraged to publish it. I just now recalled the conversation I had with the Fairy God-Mother. Before I left, we had talked of me returning and showing her the manuscript. She was to look it over and be sure I'd presented the Fairy Kingdom as per her approval. How could I have forgotten that? Just then I heard ever so softly, "Jester. Jester. Over here." 'What? Was I dreaming? Was I imagining this?' Louder now, I heard. "Jester. Over here." 'Was that Lillian's voice?' "Over here where," I said aloud. "By your ink pot on your desk," she replied. I looked down and there as beautiful as ever was Lillian, my best of all friends. Her lavender outfit as cute as I remembered it. "Oh, my gosh! Lilian! Lillian!" I cried aloud. Tears of surprise and joy were already flowing down my cheeks. "Is that really you? I'm not dreaming, am I?" "No, Jester. It's me. Look." Up she flew. Now she was directly at my eye level, a few feet in front of me.

'Oh, my God, thank you. Thank you,' I thought to myself. My heart was pounding wildly with excitement and surprise. I was too stunned to speak. I just stared at her flying about in front of me. Finally, I spoke. "Lillian, how are you? How did you find me? How did you get here? Why are you here?" All my questions came tumbling out one after another. "I am so happy to see you. I can hardly believe it!" I got up from the desk and started prancing around, exclaiming, "Lillian's here. She's really here!" The joy I felt was bubbling over in my heart. My body required movement. "I've missed you so much Lillian. I didn't know if I'd ever see you again. I finished the book. I'll show you later. First, tell me all about you and the other fairies." I sat back down to listen. The initial shock and surprise was starting to wear off. "We are all well, Jester. I've been sent by Fairy God-Mother to assist you. We have 'felt' you stuck on your path with this book. As to 'how' I found you, I had only to connect with you in my heart while Fairy God-Mother blessed me with her Magical Crystal Sphere. I will talk with you on those more serious topics later. First, let's go out and greet the morning sun. Out to your beautiful garden," Lillian concluded. "Yes. Yes," I reply. "I'll gather up some fruit for us to nibble on. Follow me." I arose from my chair and led the way to the kitchen. A few minutes later we went out back to the chairs in the garden. Prepared breakfast fruit was brought with us. "Oh, your flowers are so beautiful," Lillian exclaimed. "They remind me of you – of all of you. I spend a lot of time in this garden," I explained. I sat down in the garden chair, taking a bite of a ripe peach. The juices dripped down my chin. Lillian sat on the arm of the chair next to me, eating from the dish of tiny pieces of fruit I'd prepared for her. 'What a magical day this has turned out to be,' I thought. 'Thank you, God. Thank you!'

Lillian and I spent the afternoon catching up on all that had happened in both of our lives this past year. I was so very happy and excited to be with Lillian again. I listened intently as she spoke about the other fairies and their activities. Before we knew it, the afternoon had passed. "Are you able to stay overnight?" I asked Lillian. "I'm actually allowed to be here a few days," Lillian responded. "We've got some more work to do, you and I, with your story. Fairy God - Mother has granted permission for me to assist you." Over the next several days, Lillian and I had many wonder-filled moments together. She shared with me her amazing perception of the world. My eyes and my heart began to open up in ways I never knew existed. Colors seemed richer and smells more heavenly. Lady bugs became our constant companions. Lillian was fascinated with them and they with her. Apparently, they did not have any in the Fairy Kingdom. One evening, as we watched the sunset, Lillian spoke to me with passion in her voice. "If there is one thing we could have all living beings know and understand, it would be for them to realize that they are <u>never</u> alone. Everyone comes to this planet Earth with either a guardian angel or a spirit guide and often both or even more than one. They are here to support and guide you in any way they can. Their hope is that as a you develop and grow spiritually, you will come to be more aware of them, develop a relationship with them, asking for advice and guidance. They are better able to assist when asked in prayer for their help. For we live in an energy field of free will so they cannot intervene unless they are asked (unless of course it is to protect you from harm.) Only then are they allowed to intercede uninvited." Lillian was speaking to me up close. I could hear her speaking directly in my ear. She had so much more she wanted me to write about that she had asked me to add in another section. She believed the people were ready to listen – that in fact they were eager to learn and understand.

"The second thing I would want people everywhere to fully grasp and know with utmost certainty, is that THEY ARE LOVED!" My own wish had always been just that - that people would live their lives knowing these two things: They are never alone. They are loved. Now here, Lillian was speaking about it. Lillian continued," If human beings everywhere across the planet, lived from these two truths, the world would be a peaceful haven. For there would be no fear, no doubt, no insecurity, no anger, nor jealousy or shame or regret. All these unhealthy, negative qualities arise and are given energy when people forget from whence they came. We are all beings of Divine Energy, a Universal Energy of Light and Love. Within each of our hearts lives a flame, a Light, if you will, a Divine Spark. Our true purpose here is to discover that Light and then to nurture it and allow this Light, our true Essence to shine forth. As we learn to live our life from this Inner Light that dwells in our hearts, our daily actions sends out ripples of Love and Light across the Planet. We emanate a higher vibration that is felt and experienced by all. This in turn affords others the opportunity to do the same. The Planet Earth is in a delicate balance right now. That is why it is so important to get out this book Jester. The more people that believe in these truths, the better chance Planet Earth has of becoming the Peaceful Loving World she was created to be." I sat back in my garden chair, the sunset now forgotten. I was too absorbed in what Lillian was saying. I had used the book to encourage people to continue to believe in the miracles and the magic of life. Things that they already know 'in their hearts' to be true. Now, I was to write of these deeper yet simple truths. How was I to get people to listen, to truly listen?

One evening, my seven year old grandson, Aidan came for a sleepover. This event had been planned weeks prior. With all the excitement of Lillian being here, I'd completely forgotten. The doorbell rang and there was Aidan, with a now toothless smile. My daughter waved from the car. "Come in. Come in." I said to Aidan. "Looks like you've lost a tooth." "I did, Grandma. Just today, at school. I have it in my pocket, wrapped in a tissue. Mom says if I put it under my pillow tonight, the tooth fairy will come. That they will take the tooth and leave me something in exchange." "Wow! That is exciting, Aidan. We will definitely do that then," I replied. "Now, how about I cut you up an apple to eat. That will hold you over until supper's ready." As Aidan got off his back pac and coat, I got out an apple from the fridge. While I was cutting it, I was wondering where Lillian was. Since I had not remembered about Aidan's visit, Lillian and I had not discussed how we would handle this situation. I was reaching up for a small bowl for Aidan's apple, when I caught sight of Lillian atop of the fridge. She was smiling joyfully as she watched Aidan. She was half hidden behind a framed photo that was there. "I've got a movie I think you'll like, Aidan. One I'm sure you haven't seen. I'll get it set up and we can enjoy it together while we eat supper." A few hours later, Aidan was tucked into bed. We had washed his tooth and wrapped it nicely in a clean tissue. He placed it under his pillow, excited and curious at what the morning would bring. As I walked into the kitchen to make my evening chamomile tea, Lillian flew by and landed on the counter. "Tooth Fairies are real too, Jester," she said. "People rarely see them though. Even parents think it's only a childhood fantasy. However, Tooth Fairies are just as real as I am," Lillian explained. I looked straight at her. "Are you kidding me? Tooth Fairies are real? You mean there is such a thing?" My mind was rapidly trying to grasp what Lillian had just said. 'Why not?' I thought to myself. I know now for certain that fairies exist. Why couldn't there be 'Tooth Fairies' as well.' "Does this mean one really will come tonight – to see Aidan and take his tooth?" I asked Lillian. "Yes," she replied. "Absolutely! This is indeed a blessing for you, as well. Now, you will have an opportunity to see one. While you were busy with Aidan tonight, I was in contact with Jeramiah. He'll be the tooth fairy coming to visit Aidan tonight. I explained to Jeramiah about who you are and the relationship you now have with the Fairy Kingdom. He has agreed to be seen by you." "Really? I'll meet a real live Tooth Fairy tonight? Are they a lot like the fairies I saw when I visited you – in shape and size, I mean?" "Actually, they are even smaller," Lillian explained. "About half our size. They are also more iridescent, making it even harder for human eyes to see them." I was sitting with my tea at the kitchen table conversing with Lillian. I was filled with awe and wonder at this new information. "Why do the Tooth Fairies come to collect the children's baby teeth?" I asked aloud. Lillian explained," First of all, the term 'tooth' fairies is actually a nickname of sorts. Generations ago, people, for example, the Native American Indians were more in tune with nature. They understood about animal spirits and plant energy. They also witnessed the existence of fairies. Such experiences and wisdom gathered was passed down to the younger generations by word of mouth. Over time, as technology came to the forefront, people began to view these 'passed down' stories as just that- 'stories.' They no longer saw them as truths. Much wisdom and knowledge was forgotten. Fairies, as you know, took their Kingdom, 'underground' so to speak. Mothers, however, with their Feminine Energy and innate connection to Mother Earth, still wanted their children to 'believe.' Hence, the ritual of putting the baby teeth under the pillow, has continued." Lillian explained further," The tooth fairies, as you call them, love little children. They absolutely adore them. Loosing these baby teeth is like moving through a door into childhood. The Fairies come to visit the little ones in their sleep – to remind them of the existence of fairies." Lillian stopped abruptly. "Oh, Jeramiah, you're here," she exclaimed. "Yes, indeed. I've been listening to you two talking. Hello, Jester or should I call you Pamela? I'm Jeramiah. Speaking of nicknames, I'm sure there is a story behind that one." "Where are you?" I responded, eager to match the voice to the tiny being. "I'll move closer. In a shadow is best. You can then see my sparkling wings. How about now? Look at the shadow your tea cup is making on the table." Jeramiah explained. "Oh, there you are! My goodness, you are a tiny thing aren't you?" I blurted out. My eyes took in the tiniest of fairies. He was looking so grown up in his vest and boots. "I'm actually very strong," Jeramiah replied. "And so are my wings. I'm able to crawl under the child's pillow and gather up their tooth and carry it away." "Then what do you do?" I asked. "We say a prayer and blessing for the child. We often see a family member come in. They leave a little money under the pillow, a human tradition apparently." Jeramiah answered. "What do you do with the tooth?" I continued with my questions. "We grind it into powder and use it in our gardens," Lillian piped up. "The main point of our visit," Jeramiah explained, "is the blessing and prayer made over the child during this special time of transition from babyhood. You see, not only are we there, but also the child's Guardian Angel and Spirit of Light (or some say Spirit Guide.)" Jeramiah continued, "We impress upon the child's subconscious mind that they are loved and that they are never alone. Lillian spoke to you about these truths earlier." "It's time for me to go," Jeramiah concluded. "I already visited with Aidan while you were having your tea earlier." Then, just as abruptly, he was gone. "He's got a busy schedule tonight," Lillian explained. (I'm sure to offset my mouth gasped open still at Jeramiah's sudden exit.) "Oh, I never thought of that," I weakly replied. I sat in silence for a while. So much had happened. My mind was still attempting to absorb it all. "It's late. I'm going to retire for the night now. I know Aidan will be up early tomorrow. I think for now Lillian we'd best keep your presence hidden from him. I'll see you in the morning. Good night, Lillian." "Good night, Jester," she responded. As I climbed the stairs to bed, I knew Lillian would settle herself amidst my ornamental Fairy Village. I had created one on my living room table top. She quite enjoyed 'hanging out' there. Her other favorite spot was in my den where I did my writing. I had many stones and crystals there. She especially liked the large amethyst one. I'd often find her sitting within it. I awoke the next morning, thinking of Lillian. She'd be leaving soon. I always felt sad when I thought about that inevitable moment. I'd come to love having her around. As if reading my thoughts (well actually she probably was) Lillian appeared directly in front of my eyes. "Yes, I shall be leaving soon, Jester, tomorrow in fact. Let's go outside and greet this beautiful day. Looks like Aidan is sleeping in after all. I'll meet you guys out there." Lillian said as she flew out the bedroom door. I got up and dressed and headed down to the kitchen.' I'll just let Aidan sleep,' I thought. 'He'll find us outback.' I stopped in the kitchen long enough to make my morning tea. "Wow! It is a beautiful morning," I exclaimed as I opened the back screen door. The morning sun was drying the dew off the leaves and chairs. The smell of the flowers was 'heavenly.' The birds in the distant trees were singing their morning songs. It was indeed on its way to becoming another beautiful day on this amazing planet Earth. Sometimes, when I pause to think about all the varieties of flowers and animals and crystals and people and fruits and vegetables, I am awestruck. The word 'magnificent' comes to my mind. I think of how Heaven truly is here on Earth. Think of the rainbows and the Northern Lights and butterflies. What a spectacular planet indeed! I turned excitedly to share my thoughts with Lillian. At first, I couldn't see her in the garden. Then, lo and behold, as I followed the sound of her soft tiny voice, I spotted her. From a distance, they both looked like statues, or ornaments, like I have in my living room. On closer inspection, I realized that Lillian was deep in conversation with a rather regal looking frog! He sat so upright and towered over her. His gaze was fixed on her in awe and wonderment. 'What could they possibly be discussing,' I wondered aloud. I didn't want to disturb them, so I held back and observed this curious sight from a distance. "Grandma. Grandma," I heard Aidan calling for me. "Out here, sweetheart. I'm out back." I yelled out. Aidan burst open the screen door and ran down the steps towards me. "My tooth is gone, grandma. Look what the tooth fairy left for me," Aidan exclaimed. There, in the palm of his hand, was the tiniest of wooden sculptures. It looked just like Jeramiah! I looked over at Lillian. She must have done that last night. Amidst all the excitement of meeting Jeramiah, I'd completely forgotten about leaving the traditional money under Aidan's pillow. "Oh, Aidan," I exclaimed. "It's beautiful."

LIFE IS A MIRACLE

I was so excited. I'd made up my mind. Both my mind and my heart were telling me it was time for me to return to the Fairy Kingdom. I had recently finished the second section of the book about fairies. I now wanted to show my writings to the Fairy God-Mother. As agreed upon, before I left, almost two years ago now, I was to show them to her for a final approval before publishing. 'I'll set out first thing tomorrow,' I said aloud to myself as I crawled into bed that evening. I immediately thought of Lillian and our last visit. Lillian was my very best friend in the Fairy Kingdom. It was she who agreed to show me around when I first arrived so long ago. 'It sure will be great to see her again,' I thought to myself as I switched off the lamp by my bed. 'How will I ever be able to sleep?' I awoke early the next morning. I packed a light snack and I headed for the forest. My heart was pounding with excitement. My pace was brisk. 'What if I can't find them? What if they've moved?' My mind raced with all sorts of possibilities. Yet, as I walked further along, my mind quieted. I could feel my heart expanding. I felt stronger and more confident. I had a sense that this second visit with the fairies would, in fact, be the content for the third and final section of the book.

I had received a 'channelling' that morning that this would be so. At times, friendly Spirit Guides honor me with a visit. They wake me up, asking me to reach for pen and paper. They tell me they have something to say. My role is to 'allow' them to write. The content is always positive and uplifting. I am very grateful and honored whenever they come to visit. Of course, they showed up the night before my 'expedition.' Actually, earlier in the evening, I was sorting out some papers and I found a channelled writing from April, 2013, exactly two years ago. It spoke of me writing a book and getting it published. That was right before the day I stumbled upon the Fairy Kingdom. Now, here I was two years later, about to return to the fairies, with such a book in my hand. It all seemed rather surreal. It is so amazing how our lives can suddenly open up like that and take off in a whole new direction. I awoke about 4 am this morning. I was 'told' to open up my heart and to be willing to be vulnerable in my sharing in this final section of the book. I was also told that I would indeed be 'assisted.' I was to open up fully to my time and my experiences once again in the Magical Fairy Kingdom. 1 was to allow into my heart what they had to teach me. My, oh my, such strong messages did indeed prelude my journey. I pondered on all of these things as I walked along the forest path.

Then I heard them – the crickets. Their chorus of song engulfed me. I recalled hearing somewhere that when they slowed down the crickets' noise, it sounds just like a chorus of monks singing songs of praise. Now, I think of that every time I hear them. I paused for a moment, on the path, closed my eyes and let their sounds of praise wash over me. As I carried on, I began to think about recent prayers of mine. My life experience has shown me that every prayer is answered. A recent example was the car I just received. As we were signing the Bill of Sale, I turned to the previous owner and told her, 'You are the answer to my prayers.' Being a spiritual person herself, her eyes immediately welled up with tears. She knew exactly what I meant. Needless to say, when it was time to leave, we were all exchanging hugs like old friends. We recognized that indeed we are all connected in this Divine tapestry called life. Now, that leads to another vital ingredient in my life – Faith – Absolute Unwavering Faith. Like I wrote about earlier, we are never alone AND we are loved. Knowing that to the very core of my being assists me in living my life with Faith. That sure helps me to be patient and stay optimistic while waiting for things to unfold 'all in God's timing' as they say.

'Wow, my mind sure is going a mile a minute,' I thought to myself. It was time to get out of my head and start paying attention to where I was in the forest. I definitely did not want to miss that particular spot where I had fallen asleep last time. Then I had awoken to the fairies voices. As I walked along, I thought about how incredibly magical my life had become. 'I love my life,' I shouted aloud. The very next instant, I heard Lillian's voice. "Well, hello stranger. About time you showed up. I've been waiting for you. I knew you'd come today. I just knew it," Lillian exclaimed. "I've come to fly beside you. We can visit along the way. How is Aidan?" Lillian, had come to visit me in my world a few months ago. My grandson, Aidan had showed up unexpectedly. Lillian had observed him from a distance. "His new tooth is growing in now," I replied. "What a wonderful surprise to meet you here along the forest path. I've been thinking of so many different things today as I've walked along." "I know," replied Lillian. "I have felt you approaching, busy in your mind." "Does Fairy God-Mother know I'm coming? Does she feel me approaching also?" I asked. "Yes indeed," Lillian responded. "It was she who suggested I fly out to meet you here. We are all excited about your return." "I was so excited last night, I hardly slept," I continued. "My Spirit Guides also woke me and spoke to me about this visit back to the Fairy Kingdom." We were moving along the forest path conversing when I noticed something shiny up ahead. As we got closer, I realized it was a tin can.

"Why do people do that —drop their litter on the ground? Planet Earth is our home. Do these people drop their cans on their kitchen floor?" I expressed aloud my frustration. "I just don't understand that." "When I was walking down by the ravine on my lunch break this week, I again found some cans. They'd been just tossed there by people out for a walk. How rude is that? I picked them up and carried them back." "The fairies are so very grateful when humans take the time to pick up any litter they see," Lillian responded.

"Let's stop here. I need to rest for a bit," I said as I sat down upon a large rock located just off the path. "I love rocks and crystals. You saw my collection when you came for your visit." "I adore the amethyst necklace you are wearing now and your clear quartz bracelet," Lillian replied. "All things are energy. These crystals that you wear or carry in your pocket add positive energy to your Sphere of Light that surrounds you. Each stone is unique in its properties. So depending on what is wanted and needed, you can choose your stone for the day accordingly," Lillian explained. "Don't you just love that," I replied. "How Planet Earth assists and loves us in so many ways." I reached in my pocket. I often carried with me or wore an amulet made of rose quartz crystal. This one was especially dear to me for it reminded me of my mother. She'd gone to see a psychic once who told her that was her stone and that she should wear it often. Rose quartz is a heart stone. As I sat on the rock, I closed my eyes and allowed myself to feel the warmth of the sun's rays on my face. I thought of my parents, both now deceased. Yet, in my heart, they are still so much a part of my life. I truly believe that death is but a doorway to another realm. I often 'feel' my parents still with me. There have been times when I'm drawn to go into a store. I'll then go 'automatically' to a specific aisle. There I'll find just the right item that is a link between them and me. I call those my "Hello From Heaven" moments. An example, is when I found a 'stuffed toy Daschund!' I never knew there even was such a thing. My parents always had a daschund. These 'occurrences' often happen around special occasions, like the anniversary of their passing or Mother's Day or birthdays. If I could pass along a message to people who have just lost a loved one, it would be: Do not despair/The love you share/Is always with you/ and so are they!

I opened my eyes again. "Okay, Lillian, time to carry on. Let's share this peach along the way," I said as I stood up and reached in my bag. "You know what else I love, Lillian?" I said. "Is when I'm guided to be in the right place at the right time doing precisely the right thing for the highest good of all. In fact, I have a daily affirmation that states just that. Like the other day, I was 'prompted' to stop at a store. It turns out they had exactly what I was looking for and it was on sale! I just love when that happens! When it does, I always say thank you. Thank you for all the prosperity that continues to flow into every area of my life. I am so grateful for all parts of this journey called life. I am especially grateful for learning that I am the creator of my life. I decide what my life will be like by how I think and how I choose to feel. It's really quite amazing how the power of our thoughts works like a magnet. What I think about is what I'll attract into my life." I continued, "I guess if I look at it that way, I 'created' bringing you into my life, Lillian. You've certainly seen all my fairy ornaments and the fairy village I've built. More importantly, I believe in the existence of fairies! That's another thing I've learned. What we believe to be true, will be. If I believe I'll be late for work, I am. If I trust myself to wake up at 6 am, I do." I paused a moment. Here I was rambling aloud about so many things. Probably, because I was so excited today about going back to the Fairy Kingdom. "Jester, look," Lillian exclaimed as she pointed ahead. "Oh my goodness! There's the waterfall. I'm back! I'm back!" I shouted joyfully. As Lillian flew towards the waterfall, I hurried after her. "Lillian, is it because you are with me? Is that why I can 'see' it? What I mean is, when I left last time, I turned back to take one final look at the waterfall, and it wasn't there! It was like I'd walked through an invisible veil that separated your fairy world from my people world."

I glanced over at Lillian, awaiting her reply. I so wanted to understand. Then, as I looked over at her tiny face, I knew the answer. It was right there within my question. I turned back towards the waterfall. We'd be there soon. I wasn't sure what to expect this visit. I knew my time here would be completely different. I was different! My purpose was different too! I looked ahead towards the waterfall. Regardless of the book and the work involved, I was still excited to be back. Who wouldn't be? Here I was, once again, about to enter into the Fairy Kingdom! It was so beautiful here. The water cascaded down from one ledge to another until it came to the last drop, creating the largest waterfall. Lush, green plants and trees grew abundantly along the water's edge. As I drew closer, I saw Fairy God-Mother. Her open wings held her above the last and largest pool of water. She appeared suspended there beside the large waterfall. She was holding her Magical Sphere out in front of her, towards me, in greeting. I could feel waves of love surrounding me. "Lillian, look. There's Fairy God-Mother. She's by the waterfall," I exclaimed. "She's come to greet us." I felt so incredibly happy. My heart was full of such joy. Lillian was beside me. Fairy God-Mother was just ahead. 'How blessed am I!'

"Greetings, Pamela!" "Hello, Lillian! Welcome! Welcome!" Fairy God-Mother shouted out to us as we approached. "Come join me over here, on this large rock at the base of the waterfall." Fairy God-Mother flew over to the large rock. Lillian did the same. I walked along the water's edge. Then, using rocks as stepping stones, I made my way to the large rock also. The spray from the waterfall felt cool and refreshing. I pulled out my water bottle from my bag. I quenched my thirst before I spoke. "Fairy God-Mother, I am so grateful and honored to be here with you again. Thank you for allowing me to visit once more in the Fairy Kingdom." "She certainly has been excited," Lillian spoke up. "She's been talking and sharing about so many different things along the walk here." "Lillian told me all about her last visit with you. She described your beautiful home with all the fairy ornaments and your decorative fairy village you made. She told me about Aidan, your grandson and your visit from Jeramiah, the Tooth Fairy. Lillian tells me your book about the fairies is just about finished " Fairy God Mother spoke aloud engaging the three of us in conversation. "Yes, it is. I feel in my heart that the conclusion I'm looking for will be found within this visit. I am choosing to trust that to be so. I brought the rest with me for you to review."

I opened up my bag and pulled out my scribblers that held my rough draft. "I had a feeling you would prefer to read my original manuscript so that is what I brought," I explained. "Perfect," replied Fairy God-Mother. "Leave these with me awhile." "How about you and Lillian going off to explore? Perhaps even meet up with some of the other fairies for some fun and laughter. You and I will talk about the book later." Then, just as I was wondering if I'd get to actually 'be' a fairy size this visit, I could feel Fairy God-Mother tap the top of my head three times. I felt that familiar tingling sensation all over my body. Next thing I knew, I was sitting beside Lillian same size as her! "Oh, this is so great! Thank you Fairy God-Mother! I was so hoping I'd get to actually be a fairy again," I exclaimed. "Come on Lillian. Let's go. I so want to be 'flying' about with these wings." I jumped up onto my little feet and fluttering my wings, darted off ahead of Lillian. "Hey, wait up Jester," Lillian called after me. This was the part of my visit I always liked best. I could fly! I could fly!

The first thing I wanted to do was catch a glimpse of my reflection in the calmer waters. These were situated further away from the large waterfall where we were now. I flew towards the calmer area. I landed lightly at the water's edge. I peered over at my reflection. "Oh, Lillian! Isn't this amazing? I'm a fairy once again!" I exclaimed as Lillian set herself down beside me. "Yes, indeed, Jester, and such a beautiful fairy you are!" Lillian answered back. I admired my reflection a few minutes more. I turned this way and that, wanting to see these 'wings of mine.' Just like before, they reminded me of a dragonfly's wings. They went straight back behind me, a set of two on each side, layered atop each other. Once again, a crown of tiny bell shaped flowers adorned my head. My hair, no longer grey, was now a golden color and flowed down my back. I was in essence, the same fairy as last time. I absolutely loved this new 'body' I now inhabited. I felt so young and strong and vibrant and fully alive!! "Let's go over behind the waterfall now," I said, eager to use my wings again. Up we both arose and headed for the walkway that circled behind the falling water. "Sure is noisy back here," I yelled as loud as my tiny voice could muster. "Let's head for the cave," I added. I remembered my way to the entrance of the cave where I had first met the Fairy God-Mother. Once we were within the cave, it was easier to converse.

"Lillian, let's go down the far corridor over there," I suggested. "I always wondered from where the Fairy God-Mother had come." As we headed towards it, I glanced around in fond memory at the crystal seats. That was where the Fairy God-Mother and I had first talked and shared. I could feel my energy shifting from being surrounded by so many crystals. "Here, let me lead," Lillian said, as she flew ahead of me, turning down the corridor. Now, I would be able to see from where the corridor enters. I flew more quickly now, wanting to catch up to Lillian. Within a few minutes, we were flying out of the crystal cave and into the daylight. A large meadow stretched out before us. "Hey, this is where we played hide and seek with the flower fairies." I exclaimed. "Over there is their beautiful garden." Off in the distance, I could see the many varieties of flowers, their colors ablaze in the sunlight. I remembered so well the fun we had there. "Over the other way, Jester, is the spot from where you watched our spring Equinox celebration." Lillian added. I turned to where she was pointing. I could see the place from where I had watched the fairies build their fire that night. "So, the crystal cave is then situated between the waterfalls, which is the entrance to the Fairy Kingdom, and this large meadow," I reflected aloud.

"Yes," Lillian agreed with my summation. "Let's head over to the Fairy Village now." She continued. "We need food and water before we continue on with our day. While there we can see what the other fairies are up to." "That sounds great. Thanks again Lillian, for spending time with me," I said gratefully. "Hey, I'm your best friend, remember?" Lillian replied. "Of course, I want to be with you while you're here." We headed toward the Fairy Village situated at the farthest corner of the meadow. I looked around me in awe and wonder. 'I am here. I'm really here, back in the Fairy Kingdom once again.' I thought to myself, as we flew along. I recalled sitting in my own garden back at home over these past months, wondering if I'd ever make it back here again. I could see the Fairy Village more clearly now. Their homes, were so tiny and yet intricate. I had actually done quite a good job duplicating them for my ornamental fairy village. I had created these after my first visit. In fact, that is where Lillian had stayed when she came to visit me awhile back. Lillian spoke aloud, bringing me back to the present moment. "Let's stop and rest and get something to eat and drink." "Thank you. Yes," I agreed.

As our break was ending, we saw some of the fairies gathering close by. 'What are they up to,' I wondered to myself. Lillian, hearing my thoughts, shouted out to the group, "Hey, what's going on?" "We are getting ready for a game of Leap Frog. Want to join us?" one of the fairies replied. Lillian and I both jumped up together. In unison, we shouted out, "Yes, indeed." I had played 'leap frog' as a child. I wondered how the fairies played it. Just then, the image of an ornament I had at home, popped into my mind. I had found, at a second hand store, the cutest figurine of a smiling frog with the smallest of boys astride its back. I remembered too the large carved wooden frog I brought back from the coast last year. I had felt the most unusual 'kinship' with it. Later, as I unwrapped it at home, my heart was full of such compassion for it. It was the strangest of things. I turned to Lillian. "Are we to be playing this game with real frogs," I asked. "Oh, yes Jester. We certainly are. They are the best of playmates. You are in for a real fun time!" Lillian answered me back. We flew along behind the other fairies until they came to a grassy area beside a pond. I heard the frogs before I saw any. They make such a distinct sound. "Come out. Come out. Let's play a game. We'd love to be with you on this day," the fairies all chorused together. Only seconds later, I saw the first frog appear and then another and another.

Before long there were as many frogs as there were fairies. "Okay, form a circle please. We want to show Jester how we play leap frog," Lillian stated aloud. As if they understood exactly what she had just said, the frogs formed a huge circle on the soft grass. "Okay, Jester. I'll go first. Then, you follow me. The rest of the fairies will follow you. Here we go," she exclaimed. Lillian jumped upon the back of the frog in front of her. "Now do the same," she yelled back at me. "Oh, I don't know about this," I thought out loud. "You'll be fine. They won't hurt you. They are our friends." Lillian responded. "What if I hurt them?" I yelled back. "You won't. Come on. We're waiting on you," Lillian answered back. I flew over top and then landed myself upon the next frog's back. I immediately felt a sense of peace wash over me. It was like the frog was letting me know that all is well. I started to relax. "Okay, Lillian. I'm ready now." I yelled out to her. "Now, we form into two lines facing each other." As Lillian explained aloud to me the game, the fairies formed two lines. "Now, each fairy tries to tag the other team. If you fall off or get pushed off your frog, you're out. Whichever team has the most players at the end, is the winner."

We spent the next hour laughing and shouting in glee. Oh, what fun! I managed to stay on my frog for quite some time, surprisingly enough. The frogs were leaping here and there and everywhere. The fairies were shouting, "Go this way. Chase Lillian (or Jester or the other fairies' names.)" As the fairies stated their intention of which fairy they were aiming for, the frogs instinctively followed the necessary path. We must have made quite a sight. All these fairies astride these frogs jumping in all different directions chasing each other. Needless to say the time passed quickly. Exhausted, yet happy, Lillian and I collapsed on the grass. Our team, of course, had won! We lay their a few minutes, catching our breath. "That was so much fun, Lillian." I exclaimed. "I knew you'd like it once we started," she replied. "Bye for now, frogs. Thanks for playing," the fairies chorused their gratitude in unison. The frogs leapt their way back to the pond's edge. They then hopped back onto their lily pads to rest and bask in the sun. 'My, what a day this has turned out to be!' I thought to myself. It seemed hard to believe that just this morning, I had awoken in my own bed back home. So much had happened, all fun and miraculous! "I can hear intuitively that it is time for us to make our way back to the waterfall and Fairy God-Mother,"Lillian explained. "She is telling me that she has reviewed your manuscript and is ready to talk with you about it now."

As Lillian and I flew back towards the waterfall, I thought about the Fairy manuscript. I had written it 'from the heart,' letting it flow out of me. All was written in truth, just as I had experienced it. There was something important that I wanted to discuss with the Fairy God-Mother. Something that I had seen written on a sidewalk near my work. I had seen it recently when I was out for my lunch time walk. What I had read had troubled me deeply. "Lillian, I sense I will be saying good-bye to you soon. I feel that Fairy God-Mother will want to speak with me alone before I head for home." I turned towards my dear and special friend. I would miss her. "You are right, Jester. Fairy God-Mother does indeed seek private counsel with you," Lillian replied. "You remember, Jester, what I have said to you last time," Lillian continued. "We are connected by our love for one another. We are joined in our hearts and always shall be." I knew this to be true. "Will I ever see you again?" I asked aloud. "I don't know Jester. What I do know is that I will always remember you and the rather unusual times we had," Lillian responded. She was about to turn back. "I will always remember you too Lillian. I love you!" I shouted out as I turned to go the rest of the way on my own. Fairy God-Mother was in sight now. "I love you too, Jester," Lillian called back to me.

"Hello Fairy God-Mother," I said as I landed lightly on the rock once again. "Did you have fun with the other fairies, Pamela?" She asked. "I did indeed. We played a game of leap frog. It was great fun!" I replied. "Well, I sat here and read over the manuscript you brought. It is just perfect my child, just the way it is. Now what is it that I can feel you want to talk with me about. I can feel that something has been troubling you," Fairy God-Mother inquired. "Yes, that is correct. Let me tell you what I saw when I was out for a walk recently. It was written on the sidewalk in large letters with a blue chalk. This is what it said: Don't grow up. It's a trap! I stopped and just stared at it. I was stunned! At first I couldn't quite grasp what I was seeing. Then I continued on my walk as I was on a time schedule and needed to get back to work. As I carried on, walking briskly, back towards the office, I thought about those words. What was the person who wrote that meaning? What were they feeling? What had happened in their life to cause them to write such a thing? The ramifications were mind boggling to me. I was filled with such sadness. Then I thought of you Fairy God-Mother. I thought about this book and what I am trying to communicate with it. I thought how very sad that whoever wrote this, had already experienced, at such a young age, major disillusionments with our adult society. I wondered about the parents of this person. Had they coerced the young person to do or be something they didn't want to? Had this come as a surprise from people they trusted? Later in the day, as I pondered this some more, I thought about the important role adults have in children's lives. I thought about how young children are so trusting of the adults around them. They are trusting us to guide them on their journey to adulthood. They are trusting us to show them the way to a joyous life. They are trusting us to teach them how to achieve that goal. They are, watching how we, as adults, are living our life. They are noticing if we are happy and joyful most of the time. They can see if we are fear based people or Light filled people. They can 'feel' if we are angry people or loving people." as I concluded I looked over at Fairy God-Mother, awaiting her reply. "The answer is Love, my child. The answer for all things is always Love: Loving ourselves, loving our children, loving our planet, loving our lives. People need to see the good in each other, in themselves, and in life itself. Also, an attitude of gratitude is so very important for parents to teach their children. When we are grateful for the good in life, life in turn rewards us with even more things for which to be grateful. The parents, the aunts, the uncles, the grandparents, the friends, the corner grocery clerk, we must all be as a Beacons of Light for the children, showing them the way to success and joy. This is done by living our own lives in harmony, in peace, in love and joy. Whether it be little fairies or little people, we as adults are responsible." Fairy God-Mother had responded. We both sat in silence watching the waterfall.

"You know, Pamela, I think this book is actually a perfect response to the child's sidewalk statement," Fairy God-Mother began. "Your book is about encouraging adults and children to believe in the magic of life – like the Fairy Kingdom. You also have expressed that we are all loved and that we are never alone. You have talked about the attributes of a person who is happy, joyous and grateful. By the very act of seeing this book written and published, you are making a difference to that child's life and the lives of others." Fairy God-Mother continued, "We are all connected. Let me remind you of that, Pamela. Every time you choose love as a response to a life situation, you are helping all the children, not just Aidan." Fairy God-Mother reached over and tapped the top of my head three times with her Magical Sphere. Within seconds, I was back to my original adult form. "Come here, my child. Let me hug you good-bye." Fairy God-Mother leaned over and held me in her arms. I allowed myself to be embraced in her loving energy. I felt soothed and at peace. "I love you Fairy God-Mother," I shared aloud. "I love you too dear one," she replied. "I shall always remember you and my time here. Thank you. Thank you so much !" We both arose from the rock. It was time to part ways. I started my way across the rocks that led back to the water's edge. Once there, I turned to wave good-bye. There she was once again, embraced by the spray of the large waterfall. She raised her Sphere towards me, sending her farewell. I waved back. As I headed for the forest path, I could hear the Fairy God-Mother's voice, like a soft whisper in my ear. 'YOU ARE LOVED.'

EPILOGUE

I had returned to work. The book was complete. The last page was typed up the previous night. Then, the most magical thing happened to me. A lady approached me and asked if she could take my picture. Before she did so, she laid upon my head a crown made up of beautiful yellow flowers. Then she adorned my wrist with a bracelet made of the same colorful foliage. As she laid the crown upon my head, I felt as if the fairies themselves were 'crowning' me, in celebration for having finished the book. It all felt rather surreal. I sat there as this lady, practically a stranger, took the picture. Then she asked for my email address and said she'd send me a copy. 'That would be so perfect for the back cover of the book,' I thought. As I walked back into my office, I was in awe once again, at the Miracles and Magic that continue to fill my Life!

Thank you for reading this book. May the Universal Energy of Love and Light embrace you. May you then be a strong beacon of Light for others. Lillian and I welcome your emails. pamela.olynek@myaolcollege.com

Printed in the United States
By Bookmasters